SPACE SAVER

'To Simon'

K.A.

'To Fluff,

the sweetest, cleverest, most talented cat'

F.C.

EGMONT
We bring stories to life

Book Band: Purple

First published in Great Britain 2012
by Egmont UK Ltd
239 Kensington High Street, London W8 6SA
Text copyright © Kate Agnew 2012
Illustrations copyright © Frances Castle 2012
The author and illustrator have asserted their moral rights.
ISBN 978 1 4052 5677 3
10 9 8 7 6 5 4 3 2 1
A CIP catalogue record for this title is available from the British Library.
Printed in Singapore.
48095/1

EGMONT
Our story began over a century ago, when seventeen-year-old
Egmont Harald Petersen found a coin in the street. He was on
his way to buy a flyswatter, a small hand-operated printing
machine that he then set up in his tiny apartment.

The coin brought him such good luck that today Egmont has
offices in over 30 countries around the world. And that lucky
coin is still kept at the company's head offices in Denmark.

SPACE SAVER

Kate Agnew
Frances Castle

Blue Bananas

Things were going badly at Mission
Control. Very badly indeed.

Usually it was a great place to come to
after school. After he'd done his homework,
Ben was allowed to colour in the space
ship designs and play on the spare flight
deck until his parents finished work.

Then, on good days when the rockets were zooming nicely and everyone was cheerful, they would sometimes let him have a go in the practice space ship.

He even had his very own space suit.

Today was not a good day, though. Ben could tell that as soon as he arrived. Everyone was shouting at everyone else.

Things were so awful that nobody had remembered the biscuits for his tea.

That morning, on the far side of the moon, a wheel had fallen off the brand new spy camera's special Moon Buggy.

The astronauts couldn't fix it back on. Their hands were just too big to manage the tiny little screws that held the wheel in place.

That meant they hadn't been able to finish taking the new photos for the Spy Chief.

The buggy was so big and the new camera was so heavy they couldn't move them at all.

Now the buggy and the camera with the photos on it were all stuck on the far side of the moon. The astronauts were coming home without them.

That was why everybody was in such a terribly bad mood.

Commander Ross was in charge of
Mission Control. She was very fed
up indeed. The Spy Chief had been
shouting at her all afternoon.

'We can't just leave our special spy camera behind,' he yelled. 'Someone might steal it and look at all the pictures.' He was very angry.

'I don't think that's very likely,' said Commander Ross, but she looked a bit worried.

Ben's dad was fed up. He'd been trying to use the remote control robot from the

spaceship to fix the wheel, but its arms were too stiff to turn the screwdrivers.

Ben's mum was fed up too. She had been working on the computer for

It's not working!

ERROR! DOWNLOAD FAILED

hours, trying to find a way to download the photos while the camera was still on the moon.

Ben sat under the Command Deck to keep out of the way. He got his school project out of his bag and started on his homework.

The red telephone on Commander Ross's desk began to ring. It was very noisy in Mission Control and everyone else was busy, so Ben answered it.

'This is the Prime Minister speaking,' said a loud voice at the other end. 'And I am Very Cross.'

'That camera has some Top Secret photos on it. We can't just leave them behind. And it was Very Expensive. The Queen will be furious. I expect you to sort this problem out straight away. Do you understand?'

'Yes, sir,' said Ben. He put down the phone. 'Sssssssssh,' he shouted. The room went very quiet.

'That was the Prime Minister,' he told them all. 'He says I have to sort things out as soon as possible. Is that OK with you?'

The Spy Chief still looked very angry and Commander Ross seemed a bit surprised.

'Actually,' said Ben's dad, 'that's quite a good idea. Your hands might be small enough to turn the screws, even in your gloves.'

Ben's mum looked as if she might be about to say something, but Commander Ross spoke first.

'Brilliant!' she said. 'You'll know what
to do, won't you? You've been in the
practice ship enough times.'

Ben thought. He'd never actually gone into space before, but he'd practised a lot and he had always wanted to. 'Yes,' he said, 'I know what to do.'

'Great. We've got a rocket leaving in two hours. Can you be ready for that?'

Ben felt quite scared but Dad said it was fine, Ben knew all there was to know about rockets. Luckily his space suit was washed and ready to go.

Mum looked quite worried when it was time for Ben to board the spaceship, but the other astronauts seemed friendly.

Their spaceship was a comfy old rocket just like the practice one, so Ben thought he'd be OK.

Ben strapped himself in and Pete and
Paul flicked switches and pressed buttons.

'Don't worry, Mum,' he said. 'I'll zap
you a message when I get to the moon.'

Commander Ross began the countdown.

10, 9, 8, 7, 6, 5, 4, 3, 2, 1, lift off!

As the Earth got smaller and smaller in the distance Ben checked his tool kit to make sure he'd brought everything he might need. It was going to be a difficult job mending the buggy wheel and he didn't want anything to go wrong.

Pete and Paul, the astronauts, helped him go through the plan.

'It's going to be tricky,' said Pete.

'But you can do it,' Paul added.

Ben wasn't so sure, but Paul cheered him up, telling him exciting stories about life in space. Then Pete gave him strange ice-cream out of a shiny silver packet. It wasn't very nice, but Ben didn't want to be rude so he ate it anyway.

After that Ben tried to have a sleep. His mum had told him to make sure he had a good rest before his big adventure, but it was hard to sleep in zero gravity.

He must have dozed off though, because when he woke up Ben could see something huge and grey out of the spaceship window. It was heading towards them fast.

'That's the moon,' Paul told him.
'Fasten your seatbelt, we're coming
in to land.'

It was a bumpy landing and it made
Ben's stomach feel quite uncomfortable,
but he was so pleased to be there he
didn't really mind. When he looked out
of the window he thought he could see
the Moon Buggy in the distance.

31

Ben sent his mum a quick message and pulled on his moon-walk suit. He was ready to get to work.

'Hey,' said Paul, who was having trouble with one of his boots.
'Slow down a minute.'

But Ben was too excited to wait.
He scrambled out of the space ship
after Pete as fast as he could.

The moon felt all powdery under his space
boots and the ground was very slippery.
There were big boulders everywhere,
but at least it was easy to leap over them.
Ben and the astronauts hopped and
jumped their way to the Moon Buggy.

The camera on top of it still looked very new and shiny. 'Hmmmn,' said Pete, looking at the broken wheel. 'It looks very fiddly. Are you sure you know what to do?'

Ben had a quick look. It seemed to be just the same as the Moon Buggy he was allowed to play with at Mission Control.

'I think so,' he said, but his hands were shaking so much it was hard to open his tool kit. 'Oh dear,' he said. 'Sorry. I've never done this with my gloves on before.'

Be careful, Ben

Pete looked fed up, but Paul smiled
at him.

'Go on, ' he said. 'You can do it.'

Pete sighed, loudly.

Paul went on, 'Just give it your best
shot. Here, I'll hold your tool kit.'

Ben took out the smallest screwdriver in the kit and held it up to a screw. It looked as if it would fit. He lifted the first screw up to the buggy wheel and tried to turn it.

Try as he might, he just couldn't get the screw to turn. He tried with his left hand, but nothing happened. He tried with his right hand, but nothing happened. He put some oil on it and tried again, but still nothing happened.

'It's no good,' he said. 'I can't do it either.'
He sniffed a bit. 'Sorry,' he added.
'That's OK,' said Paul. 'At least
you tried.'

38

'Hold on a minute,' said Pete. He was looking at the tool kit. 'Why don't you have another go with this?' He handed Ben the second smallest screwdriver.

Ben took the screwdriver. It looked a bit too big, he thought. Carefully he held it up against the screw. Perhaps, just perhaps, it would still work.

Pete and Paul held the wheel up against the buggy. Slowly, Ben pushed the screwdriver into the screw.
It fitted.

Ben held his breath. Keeping his hand as steady as he could in his bulky gloves, Ben tried to turn the screwdriver.

Once, twice, three times he tried, and
on the third go the screw began to move.
'Hooray!' shouted Paul.
'Keep still!' Pete told him crossly, but he
said, 'Well done,' quietly to Ben.

Ben smiled a smile that stretched from one side of his space suit to the other. He felt like jumping up and down too, but that might have knocked the screws.

Slowly and steadily he worked on the wheel, turning the screws carefully one by one until he had fixed it tightly back on to the Moon Buggy. By the time he'd finished, it looked as good as new.

Ben jumped up and down. 'Hooray!'
he shouted. 'I've done it!'

'Fantastic,' said Paul. 'Now we'll be
able to finish taking the pictures and
get them all home safely.'
'What a relief!' added Pete.

Pete and Paul climbed into the Moon Buggy and got the camera into position, ready to start taking photos. Ben checked the screws on the camera as well, just to be on the safe side.

'There,' he said. 'It's all ready.' Ben felt proud of himself. He'd done a good job.

'Splendid,' said Pete, looking at the time dial on his space suit. 'Hop up. We should be finished by lunch-time. Then we can go home.'

'Can't we have just a few more minutes first?' Ben begged. 'I might not come back here till I'm grown-up and I really want to do some moon-walking.'

Paul smiled at Ben. 'I reckon you'll be back sooner than that,' he said. Then he winked at Pete. 'It looks like we're going to be a while,' he said. 'Shall we zap his mum and let her know?'

'You zap his mum,' Pete told Paul. 'I'm going to zap Commander Ross. I think she'll be very pleased to hear from us.'

Commander Ross
was very pleased indeed.
So were Ben's mum
and dad.

The Spy Chief and the Prime Minister
and even the Queen were all delighted too.

But nobody was as happy as Ben,

bouncing high on the far side of

the moon.